SCOOBY-DOO!

THE TERROR OF THE BIGFOOT BEAST

Curious
Fox

First published in this format in 2015 by Curious Fox,
an imprint of Capstone Global Library Limited,
7 Pilgrim Street, London, EC4V 6LB
– Registered company number: 6695582

www.curious-fox.com

The moral rights of the proprietor have been asserted.

CAPG32599

Originated by Capstone Global Library Ltd
Printed and bound in China by RR Donnelley Asia

ISBN 978 1 78202 110 0
18 17 16 15 14
10 9 8 7 6 5 4 3 2 1

A CIP catalogue record for this book is available
from the British Library.

SCOOBY-DOO!

THE TERROR OF THE BIGFOOT BEAST

written by
Laurie S. Sutton

illustrated by
Scott Neely

THE MYSTERY INC. GANG!

SCOOBY-DOO

SKILLS: Loyal; super snout
BIO: This happy-go-lucky hound avoids
scary situations at all costs, but he'll do
anything for a Scooby Snack!

SHAGGY ROGERS

SKILLS: Lucky; healthy appetite
BIO: This laid-back dude would rather
look for grub than search for clues,
but he usually finds both!

FRED JONES, JR

SKILLS: Athletic; charming
BIO: The leader and oldest member
of the gang. He's a good sport – and good
at them, too!

DAPHNE BLAKE

SKILLS: Brains; beauty
BIO: As a sixteen-year-old fashion queen,
Daphne solves her mysteries in style.

VELMA DINKLEY

SKILLS: Clever; highly intelligent
BIO: Although she's the youngest member
of Mystery Inc., Velma's an old pro at
catching crooks.

SCOOBY-DOO!

Bigfoot is on the loose in a local forest! Only YOU can help Scooby-Doo and the Mystery Inc. gang solve this monstrous mystery.

Follow the directions at the bottom of each page. The choices YOU make will change the outcome of the story. After you finish one path, go back and read the others for more Scooby-Doo adventures!

YOU CHOOSE the path to solve...

THE TERROR OF THE BIGFOOT BEAST

As the sun sets on a cool autumn day, the Mystery Machine rumbles over an old wooden bridge deep in the forest. **CREAK! GROAN!** The joints sound dangerous.

"Like, let me out of here. We're not going to make it across this bridge!" Shaggy cries. Both he and Scooby-Doo try to jump out of the van.

"Hold on, guys. It's just a little rickety," Velma assures them. She turns to the frightened hound. "Will you stay for a Scooby Snack?"

"Rou ret!" Scooby barks as he settles back into his seat.

Velma pulls out a big box of dog treats.

Turn the page.

Velma tosses one to Scooby. ***CHOMP!*** He catches the treat in his mouth and quickly gobbles it down.

She throws a treat to Shaggy, and he does the same thing as Scooby-Doo. ***CHOMP!*** They lick their lips with slobbery tongues.

Daphne looks at the map with a big red X marking their destination.

"We're almost at the cabin," she says.

"That's good, because this road is getting rough," Fred says. The Mystery Machine bounces as its tyres hit a hole in the road.

Velma bumps her head on the roof of the van. "Ow! Remind me, why are we going there?" she asks the gang.

"We're supposed to have a relaxing weekend in the woods," Fred replies. The Mystery Machine thumps over another pothole. "So far I'm not feeling very relaxed."

"We're here!" Daphne says, pointing to a cabin at the end of the road.

"Let's hurry up and get inside. It's getting dark, and I think a storm is coming," Fred says.

The gang gets out and runs for the cabin. Wind rattles the tree branches like dry bones.

"I don't like the sound of that," Shaggy says nervously.

"Ri'm not afraid," Scooby declares. A dead leaf tickles his tail and makes Scooby jump into Shaggy's arms. "Rikes! A rhost!"

The cabin is dark and dusty inside.

"Hey, the lights don't work," Velma says as she flips the light switch several times. "We'd better look for a lantern or torchs."

"Tell me this isn't a setup for a scary film," Shaggy shudders.

"Um, you're not going to like this," Daphne says. "There's no food in the kitchen."

"Ahhh! Like, what else could go wrong?" Shaggy cries, throwing up his arms.

THUMP!

Turn the page.

Suddenly, something bangs against a window. Everyone jumps.

"It's just the wind, guys. No need to worry," Fred says bravely.

"Rit's a monster!" Scooby shouts. He points at the window. A shadowy shape is visible for a second and then is gone.

"Like, the wind doesn't look like that," Shaggy moans.

"I'll go outside and have a look," Fred volunteers. Velma hands him a torch. "I'll be right back."

"Those are the famous last words in every horror flick," Shaggy says. "We're doomed!"

The gang waits several minutes for Fred to return. He doesn't come back to the cabin.

"Maybe Fred's torch went out, and he's lost in the woods," Daphne suggests. "I'll go and look for him."

"I'll go with you," Velma offers.

"Scoob and I will stay here and, um, make sure the cabin is here when you get back," Shaggy says.

Daphne and Velma leave the cabin and go out into the dark forest. It's the last time Shaggy and Scooby see them.

To follow Fred, turn the page.

To follow Velma & Daphne, turn to page 14.

To stay with Shaggy & Scooby, turn to page 15.

Fred walks bravely into the woods. The torch beam barely lights up more than a metre in front of him, but he is determined to find the source of the noise. Fred doesn't see anything around the cabin. The tree branches are nowhere near the windows.

"Maybe it was just the wind," Fred concludes. **THUD!** Something bangs against the side of the Mystery Machine. Fred jumps. "What was that?!"

Fred walks over to the van to investigate. The torch flickers as the batteries threaten to die. Suddenly, he sees a large, shadowy shape moving at the edge of the trees.

"Hey, you!" Fred shouts and starts to follow the person into the woods.

Fred hopes it's a neighbour who can help with the lights in the cabin, but why doesn't the person answer? Is it even a person?

"I could be following a bear, or Bigfoot, or worse," Fred realizes. "This could be a dangerous situation."

Fred decides to turn around to go back to the cabin. Just then, the shadowy shape is right in front of him and tries to grab him!

"Yaaa! It *is* Bigfoot!" Fred yells. He drops the torch and runs.

The weak beam of the torch illuminates a huge, hairy creature chasing Fred deeper into the woods. Then the light goes out!

If Fred hides from Bigfoot, turn to page 22.
If Fred tries to outrun Bigfoot, turn to page 29.

"Fred! Where are you?" Daphne and Velma call out. There is no answer.

"How could he get lost so fast?" Daphne wonders. "He just left the cabin a minute ago."

"Look! Footprints!" Velma says as she points to marks in the soil. "The shoe print is obviously Fred's. But what's this other one?"

"It sure is big," Daphne observes. "And why is it barefoot?"

"It looks like pictures I've seen of Bigfoot footprints," Velma says. "It can't be . . ."

Daphne and Velma look at each other and shake their heads. "Naaah!"

Curious, they follow the pair of prints to the edge of the woods. Suddenly, they hear someone coming through the undergrowth and see a shadowy shape.

"Fred?" Daphne asks.

"Bigfoot!" Velma yells. "Run!"

If Daphne & Velma head into the woods, turn to page 17.
If Daphne & Velma follow a nearby path, turn to page 53.

The door creaks shut behind Daphne and Velma. Shaggy and Scooby-Doo are left alone in the dark cabin.

"Well, here we are in an old, spooky cabin in the woods. It's nothing we haven't seen in every scary film ever made," Shaggy says, trying to laugh it off. Suddenly they hear a strange clacking sound. "What's that?!"

"Rikes!" Scooby shouts.

Shaggy swings the torch beam around the room. The weak light reveals Scooby hanging from a light fixture on the ceiling. His teeth are chattering.

"Scoob, the sound is you!" Shaggy says.

"Heh heh heh," Scooby chuckles sheepishly. "Ri knew rhat."

"C'mon, pal. The batteries in this torch aren't going to last long. Let's look for some candles," Shaggy suggests.

"Rand food!" Scooby replies.

Shaggy and Scooby go into the kitchen.

Turn the page.

They look in all the cupboards for something to eat. There isn't a can, a crumb, or a candle. The only things they find are cobwebs and spiders.

"Our friend, Bruce, should have told us there wasn't anything to eat in this place," Shaggy moans. "Like, I would have brought a pepperoni pizza."

"Pizza! Rummy!" Scooby drools as visions of little pepperonis swirl around his head.

"There's only one place we haven't looked yet, Scoob," Shaggy says. "I don't really want to go there, but I think we're desperate."

They look at the cellar door nervously.

If Shaggy & Scooby open the door, turn to page 24.

If Shaggy & Scooby decide to keep the door closed, turn to page 37.

Daphne and Velma sprint deeper into the woods. Bigfoot chases them, but he's too slow. The girls escape one danger, but now they face another one.

They are lost!

"Do you know where we are?" Daphne asks.

"Let me calculate our current position with the compass built into my watch," Velma replies. The needle spins and fixes on north. "I believe the cabin is north of here."

"Then let's walk in that direction," Daphne says.

The girls walk through the forest for a long time. At last they come to a dirt road.

"This should lead us to the main road," Velma concludes.

Before they reach the road, they see a building surrounded by armed guards!

If Daphne & Velma investigate, turn to page 43.
If Daphne & Velma search for the cabin, turn the page.

Daphne and Velma decide not to take a chance on being spotted by the armed guards. Rather, they want to find their way back to the cabin. They start heading back down the dirt road, but they don't get far. The bright headlights of a car are heading straight towards them!

"It's the Mystery Machine!" Daphne exclaims. She and Velma wave their arms to attract attention. The van stops.

"Fred! We're so glad to see – oh!" Daphne starts to say. Then she sees that Bigfoot is driving the vehicle.

"Get in, girls, or your friends are doomed," the creature threatens.

"Daphne? Velma? Help . . ." Shaggy moans from inside the van.

Daphne and Velma climb into the Mystery Machine. They see Shaggy and Scooby tied up in the back of the van. *VROOOOM!* Bigfoot accelerates down the road towards the building with the armed guards.

"You meddling kids! I'm taking you to my boss," Bigfoot commands.

"Bigfoot can't talk," Velma declares. She grabs its fur and pulls off a mask. "You're not a monster. You're a man!"

"Duh," the man scoffs.

"You creep!" Daphne exclaims. She takes a bottle of perfume from her purse and sprays him in the face. The man screams in pain and the van screeches to a stop. Daphne ties up the fake Bigfoot with her scarf while Velma frees Shaggy and Scooby.

"Like, your purse is an arsenal, Daph," Shaggy says.

Turn to page 40.

Shaggy and Scooby run up the cellar stairs, slamming the door behind them. The door doesn't stop the monster, who crashes through the old wood. It then lumbers through the cabin looking for Shaggy and Scooby, who are hiding in the shadows. They disguise themselves with lampshades and pretend to be floor lamps.

It works! The monster goes outside to look for them. While it has its back turned, Shaggy and Scooby run into the cellar.

"It won't think to look for us here twice. Right?" Shaggy whispers.

"Rhat ris it?" Scooby shudders.

"It kind of looked like Bigfoot," Shaggy replies. "But Bigfoot isn't real, right?"

"Rit rooked real to me!" Scooby says.

Go to page 32.

Fred decides to hide from the beast! He runs through the forest. The undergrowth is so dense that it slows him down. He can hear Bigfoot smashing through the bushes behind him.

"It's so dark I can barely see my hand in front of my face," Fred worries. "I hope that monster can't see me, either. Wait! That gives me an idea!"

Fred suddenly stops running. He smears dirt all over his face and grabs twigs and leaves. Then he crouches down and pretends to be a shrub.

I hope my camouflage works, Fred thinks. *Otherwise, I'm going to be a meal for that monster.*

The creature lumbers past Fred's hiding spot. Then it stops and looks around. Fred stays very, very still.

Think like a shrub. Be a shrub! Fred repeats silently, but he almost shouts in surprise at what he sees next. Bigfoot takes off its head! It's a man, not a monster!

"Bigfoot to Little Joe," the fake monster says into a walkie-talkie.

"Little Joe to Bigfoot. Report," a voice responds.

"That meddling kid got away. I'm going back for the others," Bigfoot says.

"Roger that. Bring them to headquarters. We'll deal with them," Little Joe replies.

Fred doesn't move a muscle until the fake Bigfoot disappears into the forest.

Turn to page 58.

Shaggy's stomach growls. It sounds like a hungry monster.

"Okay, it's decided. We're going in!" Shaggy declares. He grips the doorknob. The door opens into darkness. A weird smell comes up out of the gloom.

"Rat's rucky!" Scooby says as he waves away the stink with his paw.

The friends start down the stairs. Shaggy's hand shakes so hard that the torch beam bounces all over the place. Suddenly, it passes over something large and hairy.

"Yaaa!" Shaggy yells. Then he sees that the shape is really a bunch of furry winter coats. Shaggy sighs with relief. When he reaches the bottom of the stairs, he trips over something in the dark. The torch beam reveals a horrible, grinning face.

"Yaaa! It's a dead body!" Shaggy shouts. Then he sees it's a black plastic rubbish bag with an old Halloween mask poking out of it. Shaggy laughs at his fear.

"Ha ha! That was pretty silly of me, huh, Scoob," he says. "Uh, Scooby? Scooby-Doo, where are you?"

"Rup rhere," Scooby replies. He is in the rafters above Shaggy's head.

Suddenly, the rubbish bag lurches as if it's alive! Shaggy shrieks and leaps up into the rafters next to Scooby. He drops the torch on the floor. The weak beam illuminates a large shadowy shape. Then the batteries die and the torch goes out.

"We're doomed!" Shaggy moans.

Shaggy and Scooby wait in the dark. Nothing happens. The pals soon chuckle to themselves about being such scaredy-cats.

They drop down from the rafters, and Shaggy feels around for the torch. His hands come across some strange shapes and questionable textures, but he's not afraid anymore. At last, he finds the torch and gives it a whack to turn it back on. Standing in front of him is a huge hairy monster!

Turn the page.

"Ha ha, Scoob! You can't scare me by putting on one of those furry coats!" Shaggy chuckles.

"But, Ri'm over rhere, Raggy," Scooby says from near the stairs.

Suddenly, the monster tries to grab Shaggy.

"It's alive! Run!" Shaggy shouts.

Turn to page 20.

A shaggy shape lurches towards the Mystery Machine. It's covered in mud and twigs.

"The real Bigfoot!" the fake Bigfoot screams. "Get me out of here!"

The creature isn't afraid of the bright lights and walks right up to the van. It bangs its fists on the bonnet.

"Wow! Am I glad to see you guys!" the monster says in a familiar voice.

"It's Fred!" Daphne cries. "What happened to you?"

"Oh, the usual mystery – chased by Bigfoot, fell down a ravine, almost drowned in sucking mud," Fred replies.

"Meet Bigfoot," Velma says and points to the costumed captive. "He's an imposter."

"We'll compare notes later. Let's get out of here!" Daphne declares. Fred gets in the van and they drive away.

THE END

To follow another path, turn to page 11.

"What's happening?" Daphne asks as she and Velma run out of the cabin. Shaggy and Scooby tremble in the doorway.

"Fred! You captured Bigfoot!" Velma exclaims.

"*Fake* Bigfoot," Fred corrects her and pulls off the man's mask.

"Okay, *fake* Bigfoot," Velma agrees. "But what is he doing here?"

"I was hired to scare campers away from this area," the false monster says. "And it was working until you meddling kids showed up."

"We'll go into town and turn him over to the police," Fred says.

"Like, this has got to be the shortest holiday ever!" Shaggy suggests.

"Rank roodness!" Scooby agrees.

THE END

To follow another path, turn to page 11.

Fred runs through the woods. He can hear Bigfoot crashing through the undergrowth behind him, but he doesn't dare look back. He can barely see anything in front of him.

SPLOOSH!

Fred splashes into a stream. He almost falls in the mud. He runs along the stream, hoping it will lead him to the bridge the gang drove over to get to the cabin. It's a landmark he can use. But the stream doesn't lead him to the bridge; it takes him to the edge of a steep waterfall.

"Uh-oh! It's the end of the road," Fred says.

SPLOOSH! SPLOOSH! He hears Bigfoot splashing through the water behind him.

There's nowhere left to run!

"Geronimo!" Fred shouts as he jumps over the waterfall. He lands with a splash in the lake.

Fred swims underwater as far as he can. When he comes up for breath, he sees a light in the distance.

Turn the page.

The light is coming from a large building.

Fred reaches the shore and crawls up the muddy bank. He wishes he had stayed in the lake as soon as he sees that the building is patrolled by armed guards!

"If I thought being chased by Bigfoot was bad, this is worse," Fred realizes.

Suddenly, he sees a large, shambling shape walk out of the woods. It's Bigfoot!

Fred is startled to see the creature stroll right up to the guards and give them high-fives. Then Bigfoot walks into the building.

If Fred decides to go get help, turn to page 42.
If Fred investigates himself, turn to page 35.

"We've got to get out of here. But how do we get past big and hairy out there?" Shaggy wonders. He looks at the furry winter coats hanging by the stairs. Then he picks up the old Halloween mask. "I've got an idea."

Shaggy grabs a couple of the winter coats and climbs onto Scooby's shoulders. He wraps the coats around them and puts on the mask.

"Like, we make a pretty scary monster!" Shaggy says. "Let's see how brave this Bigfoot really is."

The Scooby monster stumbles up the stairs.

The two monsters meet face to face in the living room. With Shaggy riding on Scooby's shoulders, the Scooby monster is taller than Bigfoot. Scooby can't see under the coats and lumbers towards Bigfoot like a zombie. Shaggy raises his arms and shakes his fists at Bigfoot. Scooby-Doo growls his best growl. *GRRRR!*

"Yaaa!" Bigfoot shouts, then faints and falls to the floor. The impact makes Bigfoot's mask fall off.

"Like, it's a man, not a monster!" Shaggy exclaims. "Bigfoot is a big fake!"

Scooby peeks out from under the disguise.

"Rig rake!" Scooby says.

When Bigfoot wakes up, he is tied with a rope. Shaggy and Scooby stand nearby. So do Fred, Daphne, and Velma.

"You have a lot of explaining to do," Fred says to the man who was Bigfoot.

"You meddling kids!" the man grumbles. "I was trying to scare away campers like you."

"You're using the wrong monster," Velma points out. "Most people want to see Bigfoot. A sighting would bring people here, not chase them away."

"My boss wanted Bigfoot. That's all I know," the man shrugs.

"Who is your boss, and what's he up to?" Daphne asks.

"I'm not saying." The man frowns.

Turn the page.

"We'll take him to the authorities in town," Fred decides.

"Like, civilization! We can finally get some food!" Shaggy says.

THE END

To follow another path, turn to page 11.

"This is very strange. I'm going to take a closer look myself," Fred decides.

He creeps on his hands and knees towards the building. He is covered in mud and weeds from the lake. It's perfect camouflage.

Fred peeks into the nearest window. He sees a man sitting at a desk, working on a computer. There are maps and charts on the walls.

Then, Bigfoot bursts into the room!

The creature waves its arms in the air and stamps its feet. The man at the desk barely notices. Suddenly, Bigfoot pulls off its head!

"It's a mask! Bigfoot is a man, not a monster!" Fred gasps.

"Those meddling kids! They could ruin the whole operation," the fake Bigfoot complains. Fred can hear his muffled words through the window.

What operation? What's going on? Fred wonders. He watches Bigfoot jam his mask back on and stomp out of the room.

Turn the page.

"Hmm. What could these two be up to? I think I'll take a look around," Fred decides.

Fred sneaks around the side of the building and discovers an open warehouse. It is filled with stacks of knockoff designer shoes, handbags, and other branded products.

"They're smugglers!" Fred realizes.

Turn to page 47.

Scooby and Shaggy decide to keep the door closed. Then someone, or something, bangs on the front door. They jump in surprise.

"Like, we sure are jumpy," Shaggy says.

WHAM! Suddenly the door bursts open. A tall, shadowy shape stands outside.

Shaggy is so frightened that his hair stands on end. Scooby-Doo starts to run in the opposite direction, but his nose sniffs something yummy.

"Food!" Scooby exclaims.

"Hi, guys. It's Bruce," the shadowy shape says. "I brought groceries."

Bruce walks into the cabin with two bags of food in his arms. Shaggy and Scooby are so glad to see him that they hug him. Then they grab the groceries and rush into the kitchen.

Why is it so dark in here? Bruce wonders. He goes to the fuse box and flips the breakers. The lights go on. Then he goes into the kitchen. Shaggy and Scooby are busy making huge sandwiches.

Turn the page.

"Where's the rest of the gang?" Bruce asks.

"Like, they heard a noise outside and went to investigate," Shaggy replies through a mouth full of sandwich.

"That's never a good idea. I've seen those films," Bruce shudders.

THUMP! Suddenly, there's a loud sound from the cellar. Everyone jumps in alarm.

"Yaaa! What was that?!" they say in unison.

"Sh-should someone go and look?" Shaggy asks.

Bruce goes over to the cellar door.

"Nope," Bruce says as he locks the door and shoves the back of a chair under the doorknob. "If the films have taught me anything, it's to never go into the cellar of a old cabin in the woods."

CRASH! There's another loud sound from the cellar. The friends cling to each other and tremble. After a while, there are no more noises, and the friends relax.

"It was probably a raccoon," Bruce says.

"Like, d-does a raccoon l-look like that?" Shaggy stutters in terror. He points to a face in the kitchen window.

"Yaaa!" the three friends scream.

Turn to page 50.

"We've got to find Fred and get out of here," Daphne says as she puts the Mystery Machine into drive.

"I'm sure this fake Bigfoot is part of a bigger scheme," Velma notes.

"We'll get him to confess," Shaggy promises. He and Scooby sit on top of the man in the hairy costume.

"Reah! Ralk, mister!" Scooby growls.

"M-my boss wants to keep people away from this area," the man reveals. "He's part of a big crime family. What can I say? The pay is good!"

Suddenly, Daphne hits the brakes. **_SCREEECH!_**

Something blocks the road and their escape!

Go to page 27.

"It's not smart to take on Bigfoot and armed guards all by myself," Fred decides. "I'm going to get help."

Fred crawls along the edge of the lake towards the trees. He is covered in mud and weeds. It's damp and squishy, but he thinks it's great camouflage. Unfortunately, a territorial muskrat thinks he's a rival! The animal chatters a loud challenge.

"Shhh! I'm not going to hurt you," Fred assures the muskrat. "I'm just passing through."

The animal doesn't understand a word Fred says. It rushes towards the intruder. Fred jumps to his feet and runs. A spotlight zooms in on him.

"Freeze!" a voice booms over a loudspeaker. The guards have seen him.

"I'm doomed," Fred gulps.

THE END

To follow another path, turn to page 11.

Velma and Daphne decide to investigate on their own. They slowly begin moving towards the mysterious building. They can't be spotted by the armed guards in the distance.

"Why would a building in the middle of the woods need armed guards?" Velma wonders aloud.

"I wonder who they are," Daphne replies. "Maybe this isn't such a good idea."

Suddenly, Daphne feels a tap on her shoulder. She jumps in surprise!

"What are you girls doing here?" Fred asks. "I thought I was alone out here."

"We were looking for you when a Bigfoot monster chased us into the woods," Daphne says. "Did you see it?"

"Yes, I saw that monster too, and it disappeared into that building," Fred explains to the others.

"Why do you think that building needs armed guards?" Velma asks.

Turn the page.

"Let's come back tomorrow when it's light out and look for clues," Fred suggests.

Fred, Daphne, and Velma are about to leave when they hear the sound of a familiar engine.

VROOOOM!

"It's the Mystery Machine!" Fred says. "What's it doing here?"

"What is Bigfoot doing driving it?" Velma wonders.

"Look! They have Shaggy and Scooby!" Daphne exclaims.

Their friends climb out of the back of the van and are taken into the building.

"C'mon gang. We have to rescue Shaggy and Scooby," Fred declares. "I've got a plan."

Fred creeps through the woods towards the power generator at the back of the building. He is covered in mud and twigs and leaves so that he looks like a shrub.

None of the guards see him.

Fred goes to the master switch and shuts off the generator. The whole place goes dark.

"It's your turn, girls," Fred whispers as he sneaks back into the woods.

All the guards run around in confusion.

Daphne and Velma quickly slip into the building. They find Shaggy and Scooby in a room that looks like an office. There are maps and charts on the walls and a big desk with a computer on it.

"Like, are we ever glad to see you!" Shaggy says. "What do you think this place is?"

"That's a good question," Velma says. She studies the maps while Daphne cuts the ropes around Shaggy and Scooby.

"Let's go!" Daphne says as soon as their friends are free.

"I want a quick look at this computer. Maybe I can find a clue," Velma says.

"Make it fast! I hear someone coming down the hall," Daphne says urgently.

Turn the page.

WHAM!

Suddenly, the door bursts open and a guard rushes in.

"We're doomed!" Shaggy moans.

Turn to page 60.

VROOOOM!

Suddenly, Fred hears the sound of a familiar engine. It's the Mystery Machine!

He is surprised to see it driving up to the building. He is even more surprised to see that Bigfoot is at the wheel.

"Hey! Bigfoot took my van!" Fred says. Then he sees Daphne, Velma, Shaggy, and Scooby climb out of the back. Armed guards march them into the building. "Hey! Bigfoot took my friends!"

Fred knows that he has to rescue his pals. He needs a plan. Fred sees a couple of lorries parked nearby and decides they will make the perfect diversion. He sneaks up to the lorries and rigs the accelerator pedals and steering wheels to drive off into the woods. Fred starts the ignitions and away they go.

"That will keep them busy," Fred says as the guards chase the runaway lorries. He sneaks into the building to look for his friends. It doesn't take him long to find them.

Turn the page.

Fred bursts into the room where Bigfoot and his boss were talking earlier. He hears a *THUD* as he opens the door.

It's Bigfoot! He's sprawled out on the floor.

"Like, perfect timing!" Shaggy says.

"Are we glad to see you," Daphne adds.

"We don't have much time. Let's get out of here," Fred says as he ties up Bigfoot with a roll of packing tape.

The gang runs from the building to the Mystery Machine. The guards are still chasing the runaway lorries. No one sees them climb into the van and drive away.

"What was going on back there?" Daphne asks.

"It's a smuggling operation," Fred and Velma say at the same time.

"I saw the maps and charts on the wall," Velma explains. "They were tracking shipments all over the world. Everything is linked to something called Yeti Gomba Chatang in Tibet."

"Bigfoot was a man disguised as a monster to keep people away," Fred says. "But I wonder from what?"

"Bigfoot! Smugglers! Let's get out of here while we can!" Shaggy says.

"Not yet, guys. We've got a mystery to solve." Fred declares.

Turn to page 61.

The face in the window disappears. Shaggy, Scooby, and Bruce hug each other and shake. The front door opens with a bang.

"Rit's coming to ret us!" Scooby-Doo whimpers.

"Quick! Find something to defend yourself with!" Bruce yells. He grabs a spatula. Shaggy picks up a jar of mayonnaise. Scooby-Doo bravely shields the sandwiches with his body.

They see a human-shaped . . . thing . . . shuffle into the cabin. It is covered in mud and twigs and leaves.

"Zoinks! It's a wild man of the woods!" Shaggy shrieks.

Turn to page 52.

"Hi, guys! It's me, Fred!" he says. He wipes muck from his face. "I fell down a hill and into a pond. It took a while to find my way back here. It's a good thing the lights were on."

"Hey, the lights are on!" Velma says as she and Daphne return.

"Where have you been? It's not safe out in the woods in the dark," Bruce says.

"We were looking for Fred," Daphne replies. "And it looks like we found him!"

"Mission accomplished," Shaggy says as he carries a tray of sandwiches. "Let's start this holiday with a feast."

Suddenly, there is a loud crash on the roof.

"Yaaa! What's that?!" the friends cry.

THE END

To follow another path, turn to page 11.

Daphne and Velma scramble towards a nearby path. Bigfoot chases closely after them.

Suddenly, they encounter a deep ditch that blocks their path.

"We can't get over that," Daphne cries.

Velma points at some thick vines. "We can if we imitate Tarzan," she says.

Daphne grabs one of the long, twisting vines from the trees above. She holds on tight, takes a step back from the ledge, and starts counting. "One . . . two . . . three!" Daphne leaps from the cliff, letting out a Tarzan-like scream, "Ahhhhh!"

Velma watches her swing safely across the ditch. Then she steps up and takes her turn. "Ahhhh!" she screams, soaring to the other side.

The girls quickly hide behind a clump of bushes just as Bigfoot lands on the other side of the ditch as well. The creature paces back and forth and then takes off its head!

"Look," Daphne whispers to Velma.

Turn the page.

"That monster is a man!" Velma concludes.

RINNNG!

A loud ringing suddenly echoes through the forest. Daphne and Velma watch the man reach into a pocket of the fake Bigfoot suit. He pulls out a mobile phone and begins talking.

"I wonder who he's talking to," Daphne says.

"There's a mystery here," Velma declares. "Look at that flower over there." Velma points to a beautiful flower. "That type of orchid doesn't grow in this part of the country. It must be some kind of clue."

Soon, the Bigfoot hangs up the phone and disappears back into the woods.

"Let's see where he goes," Velma says. "It won't be hard to follow his footprints."

Daphne and Velma follow Bigfoot through the woods. The large man crashes through branches and stomps through leaves, but the girls are as quiet as possible. They are surprised when he leads them back to the cabin.

"At least we're not lost anymore," Daphne says with crooked smile.

CRAAAAAASH!!

Bigfoot suddenly breaks down the door of the cabin. The girls hear screaming and barking coming from inside.

"That's Shaggy and Scooby. They're in danger!" Velma exclaims. "We've got to help them."

Daphne and Velma sprint towards the cabin's front door, ignoring any danger. They burst inside. The fake monster is looming over Shaggy and Scooby.

"Get away from our friends, you Bigfoot bully!" Daphne shouts.

With all their might, she and Velma tackle the furry fake. The impact knocks off the man's mask. The hairy head goes flying through the air.

"Yaaaa!" Shaggy and Scooby shriek at the sight. Then Bigfoot lands on top of them. "Yaaaaa!"

Turn the page.

"What's happening? What's going on?" Fred shouts as he runs into the cabin. "Yikes! Bigfoot!"

"*Fake* Bigfoot," Daphne says as she sits on top of the man.

Velma picks up the man's fur-covered mask. She holds it in the air for all to see.

"Okay, *fake* Bigfoot," Fred agrees. "So why is this guy dressed up like that?"

"Because of this," Velma says. She pulls the petal of a flower from her pocket.

"It's a rare, night-blooming orchid," Velma explains. "I found it when Daphne and I were hiding in the bushes."

"Those flowers are worth hundreds of dollars each!" the fake Bigfoot says. "I was hired to guard a secret garden growing on the other side of that ditch."

"It's illegal to sell the plants," Velma continues. "His boss must be working in the black market."

"And we would have got away with it if it hadn't been for you meddling kids and that dog of yours," the man grumbles.

"Yay! Mystery solved!" Shaggy says.

THE END

To follow another path, turn to page 11.

"I have to save my friends from that fake Bigfoot," Fred decides.

Fred follows the man through the dark forest as quietly as he can. He hopes the sound of the wind will cover up any noise he makes.

At last, he sees the cabin in the distance. Bigfoot heads straight for it. Fred heads for the Mystery Machine and grabs a rope.

Fred lassoes the man with the rope. "Yeehaw! Git along little doggie – er, little *Bigfoot*!" he shouts.

"What? Hey!" the man yells in surprise.

Fred tackles Bigfoot to the ground and ties his wrists and ankles. "Just like in a rodeo," Fred says.

Turn to page 28.

"Run!" Daphne cries. The gang stampedes right over the guard and out of the building.

"There's the Mystery Machine!" Velma says. "Get in!"

Scooby points at the creature in the driver's seat. "Ruh-roh! Bigfoot!" he shouts.

"Don't worry. It's me . . . Fred!" their friend says. He is still disguised as a shrub. The gang climbs into the van and Fred drives off.

"There's a bigger mystery here than Bigfoot," Velma says. "That computer was full of shipping schedules and timetables. Everything is linked to something called Yeti Gomba Chatang in Tibet."

"Something tells me we're going on a trip," Fred says.

Go to page 61.

"It took a lot of searching on the Internet, but I found out what Yeti Gomba Chatang means. Yeti Gomba is a temple, and Chatang is a village in Tibet – and here we are!" Velma says.

The gang shivers in the frigid air in the land of Mount Everest.

"Like, I wish we weren't," Shaggy complains. "Why didn't the clue lead us to somewhere warm, like Hawaii?"

"Let's find a guide to take us to the temple," Fred says.

They knock on every door in town, but no one will take them to the temple. "Everyone says the temple is haunted by the Yetis," Daphne reports.

"Okay, we'll just have to find the temple on our own," Fred says.

"Like, I'm never eating an ice lolly again. Let's get out of this freezer." Shaggy moans as they trudge up a steep mountain trail.

"How about some Scooby Snacks?" Velma asks. She shakes a box of the treats.

Turn the page.

"Rum-my!" Scooby exclaims as he plows through the snowdrifts towards Velma.

RUUUUMMMMBBLE

Suddenly, there is a rumbling sound.

"Is that your tummy, Scoob?" Shaggy asks. The sound gets louder. Then the ground shakes.

"No, it's an avalanche!" Velma shouts. "Run!"

The gang splits up, trying to escape the rushing snow. *FWOOSH!* It crashes over them like a tidal wave.

To follow Daphne & Velma, turn to page 63.

To follow Fred, turn to page 64.

To stick with Scooby & Shaggy, turn to page 66.

Daphne and Velma help each other out of a snowbank and into a blinding blizzard.

"Fred! Shaggy! Scooby-Doo! Where are you?" they shout.

"I'm sure they were able to dig out of the avalanche," Daphne says. "We'll find them."

Amid the freezing temperatures, Daphne and Velma continue to search for their friends without success. But then they stumble upon an ornate building.

"Yeti Gomba! It's the temple we were looking for!" Velma exclaims. The girls rush inside.

"Jeepers, it's beautiful," Daphne whispers in awe.

Velma wanders away to study the wall paintings. Suddenly, the temple door opens with a blast of snow and wind. A shadowy shape shambles into the temple.

"Fred!" Daphne exclaims. "Where are Shaggy and Scooby?

Turn to page 67

Fred digs out of the snow and looks around. A blizzard is blowing, and he can't see.

"Daphne! Velma! Shaggy! Scooby! Where are you?" Fred shouts. No one answers. "I can't hear anything over this wind."

Fred searches for his friends. The blowing snow stings his eyes and makes it difficult to move forward. The avalanche has made the mountainside unstable. Fred can walk only a few steps at a time before he sinks into deep patches of shifting snow. He is in danger of falling into a hidden crevice, or worse.

"Oh no, have I lost my friends forever?" Fred cries.

Fred stumbles through the blinding snowstorm. He calls out for his friends. At last he sees the shape of a large building. It's a temple.

"Yeti Gomba!" Fred exclaims. "It's the Yeti Temple we were looking for."

Fred rushes up the steps to the heavy wooden door. It is twice his size and very hard to open.

Fred pushes with all his might. The door creaks inwards on rusty hinges. A blast of snow and wind follow him into the building.

"Fred!" Daphne shouts. "You're safe!"

"Daphne! Am I glad to see you!" Fred exclaims. "Oh no, where are Velma, Shaggy, and Scooby?"

Daphne points to where Velma is studying some wall paintings. Fred is happy to find at least two of his friends. But where are Shaggy and Scooby?

Turn to page 67

After a while, Shaggy and Scooby pop their heads out of the snow. They look around and see that they are in the middle of a blizzard.

"Daphne! Velma! Fred! Where are you?" Shaggy shouts. There is no answer. All he hears is the howling wind.

Scooby sniffs around in the snow, trying to smell their scent, but all he gets is a frozen nose. "Rhey're not rhere," he says.

"Maybe the avalanche missed them, and they're looking for us up on the trail," Shaggy reckons. "We'd better get back up there."

"Rokay," Scooby shivers.

The buddies start the long trek up the steep slope.

Turn to page 73.

"I thought Shaggy and Scooby were with you," Daphne says to Fred.

"I thought Shaggy and Scooby were with *you*," Fred says to Daphne.

The gang seems stumped by their missing friends, but this isn't the first time Scooby and Shaggy have become separated. Fred, Daphne, and Velma keep looking until they finally notice their surroundings.

"Wow! This place is amazing!" Velma shouts from across the vast room. "All the paintings, statues, and carvings are of Yetis!"

Fred reaches out and touches one of the statues.

CLICK!

A secret latch opens a hidden door.

CREEAAK!

"Hey! Check this out!" he tells the others.

Daphne and Velma stare into a passageway that leads into darkness.

Turn the page.

"Let's investigate!" Fred says.

"Maybe we'll find some more clues," Velma adds.

"I don't know. It could be dangerous," Daphne cautions.

Fred and Velma shrug their shoulders. Their sense of adventure drowns their sense of staying safe.

"Okay, let's go." Daphne sighs and follows her friends. "There's always the chance that the smugglers aren't using this place as a headquarters."

The passageway is very short. There is a door at the other end. Light shines around the edges of the frame.

"There's something on the other side," Daphne whispers.

"Let's take a look," Fred and Velma say in unison. They push the door open.

BANG!

The door at the other end of the corridor slams shut. There is only one way out of the passageway now – forwards. They step into the chamber and gasp at the sight!

Turn to page 80.

Shaggy and Scooby paddle as hard as they can to stay away from the whirlpool. It's no use. The vortex sucks them into its grip! They spin around and around.

Desperate, Scooby jumps into the water and drives his legs like propellers. He accelerates the cart like a speedboat. It goes so fast that they get tossed out of the whirlpool! They fly through the air and land in the water farther down the river.

"You saved us, Scoob!" Shaggy says as they float along in the gentle current.

"Ruh-roh," Scooby gulps as his ears pick up a roaring sound in the distance. They are headed straight for a waterfall.

"Not again!" Shaggy moans.

Turn to page 85.

"We get out of here and alert the authorities," Velma replies. "I'm sure my cousin in Interpol would like to know about this place."

"We'll use one of the cargo lorries to escape," Fred says. "We just have to get past those Yetis."

"Yetis?!" Daphne and Velma gasp.

Fred points to a pair of hairy monsters standing guard near the lorries. They are holding stun rifles.

"Since when do Yetis carry weapons?" Daphne wonders aloud.

"They aren't Yetis. Those are men in furry snowsuits," Velma realizes. "They're probably disguised to look like Yetis to scare away the locals."

"Just like Bigfoot back home," Fred says. "These smugglers seem to follow a pattern."

Turn to page 75.

Shaggy and Scooby stumble blindly through the blizzard. They can't see where they're going, let alone find their friends.

"It's no use, Scoob. We'll never find them in this snowstorm," Shaggy moans.

Scooby points to a large dark shadow in the mountainside. "Rut's rat?" he says.

"Like, it's a cave! We can get out of the snow. Come on!" Shaggy exclaims.

They run towards the opening. Inside, they see rusty ore carts and old equipment.

"Hey, it's not a cave. It's an abandoned mine," Shaggy realizes. *MOOOOOAAANNN!* A moaning noise races through the mine. It sounds like a tortured ghost. "Like, maybe it's not so abandoned after all."

SNIFF, SNIFF, SNIFF! Scooby's nose twitches. His whole body poses like a bird dog on point.

"What do you smell, pal?" Shaggy asks. "Have you found the gang?"

"Nope. Pizza!" Scooby-Doo replies.

Turn the page.

Scooby drools with hunger. Then he follows the scent deeper into the mine.

"Scooby! Stop!" Shaggy shouts. He picks up an old lantern and turns it on. "Like, we need some light in here."

The two friends walk into the dark mine shaft.

Turn to page 77.

"How are we going to get past the guards?" Daphne asks.

"Don't worry, I have a plan," Fred says. "First, we need to create a distraction. Everybody push this crate."

Daphne and Velma help Fred push a large packing crate until it starts to tip over.

SMASH! It crashes into a stack of crates next to it. They crash into more crates like dominoes. The guards run towards the commotion and away from the lorries.

"Let's go!" Fred says. They head for the parked vehicles.

More Yeti guards run into the loading area. Thinking fast, Fred waves his arms and shouts.

"Help! There's been a collapse in the warehouse!" Fred yells. The guards run past him and into the warehouse storage area.

"I can't believe that worked," Velma says.

"Neither can I!" Fred replies.

Turn the page.

They climb into the front of the nearest lorry.

Fred turns the ignition key. The engine sputters at first, and then it roars to life. He steps on the gas.

"Hey! Stop that lorry!" one of the Yeti guards shouts. "Nobody's allowed to leave until the blizzard is over."

Fred drives the lorry down a short exit tunnel as fast as he can. Behind him, the Yeti guards chase the lorry. Ahead of him is a large wooden door. It is closed!

If Fred slams on the brakes, turn to page 83.

If Fred crashes through the wooden door, turn to page 88.

Shaggy and Scooby reach the end of the tunnel. The weak light from the lantern illuminates a door.

"Like, that's a weird place to put a door," Shaggy says.

"Pizza!" Scooby reminds him.

Shaggy carefully opens the door. Warm air and bright light are on the other side. So are a table and chairs – and a pizza.

"Who delivers way out here?" Shaggy says, grabbing a slice. He hands a piece to Scooby. Then he hands a slice to another waiting hand.

"Thanks," a voice says.

"You're welcome, Scoob," Shaggy replies.

"Raggy, rat wasn't me," Scooby says.

Shaggy and Scooby look behind them. A huge hairy monster holds the piece of pizza.

"Yaaaa! Yeti! Run!" Shaggy shrieks.

The Yeti chases Shaggy and Scooby out the door and into the mine tunnel.

Turn the page.

Scooby and Shaggy see an ore cart.

"Jump in, Scoob!" Shaggy says. Scooby dives into the cart and Shaggy starts pushing it with all his might. The rusty wheels squeal on the tracks.

"Ret's go!" Scooby says as he pulls Shaggy into the cart. They roll down the tracks, leaving the Yeti behind.

"That was close!" Shaggy says.

"Uh, ruh-roh!" Scooby gulps and points ahead.

They are headed for the edge of a cliff!

"Where's the brake?!" Shaggy yells.

"Rhere!" Scooby shouts. He pulls a lever on the outside of the cart.

SCREEEEECH! Sparks shoot out from between the wheels and the brake. The cart barely slows down.

"We're doomed!" Shaggy moans.

"Re're gonna die!" Scooby sobs. The pals hug each other.

The ore cart stops at the brink of the cliff. Shaggy and Scooby peek over the edge of the cart at a deep, vertical shaft.

"Don't move, Scoob," Shaggy advises.

If Scooby & Shaggy stay still, turn to page 82.
If Scooby & Shaggy get out of the cart, turn to page 94.

"It's the smugglers' HQ," Daphne says. "I was right."

They are in a huge room that used to be the temple mausoleum. Coffins are stacked in niches carved into the stony walls all the way to the ceiling. The rest of the chamber is being used as a smuggling warehouse. There are stacks of crates three levels tall.

They watch workers drive forklifts to move crates from the storage facility to lorries parked in a loading area. It's a very busy operation.

"I don't know what's in those crates, but it can't be legal," Fred says.

"What should we do?" Daphne asks.

Turn to page 72.

Scooby and Shaggy stay completely still. The cart teeters on the edge of the mine shaft.

"Ahh, ahh!" Scooby gasps as dust tickles his nose.

"No, Scoob, nooooo!" Shaggy yells.

ACHOO!! Scooby lets out a monstrous sneeze. The cart plunges over the cliff!

Shaggy and Scooby fall. And fall. Until they splash into an underground river. The current is gentle, but then they hear the roaring sound of rapids.

"Ruh-roh," Scooby whimpers.

The pals almost fall out of the cart as it bounces over the rocks, but there is more danger ahead of them.

"Zoinks! A whirlpool!" Shaggy cries.

Turn to page 70.

Fred slams on the brakes! The vehicle comes to a thunderous stop. Fred, Daphne, and Velma are dazed and can't run away from the Yeti guards. They are pulled from the lorry.

"You're not going anywhere, you meddling kids," one of the guards says. "The boss said you might come snooping, and here you are!"

"You . . . you were expecting us?" Velma asks.

"Yes, especially after the trouble you caused at the Bigfoot operation," the guard replies. "We're going to lock you up for a long time."

"I told you not to go down that passageway," Daphne moans.

Suddenly, they hear a familiar cry echo off the icy cave walls. "Scooby-Dooby-Dooooo!"

They see two Yetis on snowmobiles racing towards them. The guards are so surprised at the sight that they are motionless. The snowmobiles knock them down like bowling pins. Daphne, Velma, and Fred are about to run when the two Yetis take off their masks.

Turn the page.

"Shaggy! Scooby! You found us!" Daphne exclaims.

Fred, Daphne, and Velma climb onto the back of the snowmobiles, and they drive down the mountain to safety.

"Like, it looks like it's all downhill from here!" Shaggy declares.

THE END

To follow another path, turn to page II.

"Look! There's a dry tunnel over there!" Shaggy shouts, pointing to a large opening in the rock wall. "Jump!"

The pals leap for their lives. They make it to safety just as the cart plunges over the waterfall.

"We might as well see where this goes," Shaggy says.

The pals head down the tunnel. As they walk through the dark, they hear a moaning sound. It gets louder and louder.

"Zoinks! This mine is haunted!" Shaggy says.

"Rhosts?!" Scooby whimpers.

Suddenly, they see the source of the sound. Shaggy and Scooby come to a cave where dozens of men are working, digging light blue rocks. Their groans drift down the tunnel.

"They're mining turquoise," Shaggy observes. "It's really valuable."

"Rikes! Rook, Raggy!" Scooby gulps, pointing to large hairy monsters standing guard over the workers.

Turn the page.

"Wait, those aren't Yetis. They're just guys in furry snowsuits," Shaggy realizes. "But how are we going to get past them and get out of here?"

Scooby points to a group of workers pushing an ore cart out of the cave. Shaggy has an idea. The pals disguise themselves as workers. They smear dirt on their faces and clothes and pick up some digging tools.

"It's working," Shaggy whispers as they push a cart past the guards.

"Hey, you!" a Yeti guard says to Scooby. "You're not one of the regulars."

"Run!" Shaggy yells.

"Stop!" the guard shouts and chases them.

More guards chase Shaggy and Scooby. The workers see this as their chance to escape! They run after Shaggy and Scooby, too. Suddenly, a whole mob is after the two friends.

"Zoinks! There's no way out!" Shaggy gulps as they come to a large, locked door. "We're trapped!"

But instead of being captured, Shaggy and Scooby are cheered by the workers.

"Hooray! You have freed us!" they shout. Shaggy and Scooby look confused. "These bad men forced us to dig for the blue stone. They would have got away with it if it had not been for you two strangers."

"Uh, we were just looking for our friends," Shaggy says.

"We will help you find them. Then we will all go home!" the workers declare.

THE END

To follow another path, turn to page II.

The lorry smashes through the door and zooms down the mountainside. The blizzard makes it hard for Fred to drive. He can't see where he is going. The only direction he's sure of is downhill.

"Look out!" Daphne yells and points to where the road disappears!

The vehicle sails through the air as the road vanishes. The lorry lands in a deep snowdrift far below. Fred, Daphne, and Velma crawl out of the lorry. Friendly hands and paws help them.

"Shaggy! Scooby! It's you!" Velma exclaims.

"Like, where have you guys been? We were looking all over for you," Shaggy says.

"We'll tell you later," Fred replies. "Right now we've got to get out of here. But how? The lorry is wrecked."

"I've got a plan!" Velma announces. "The lorry has a cargo of tents. We can use them to make hang gliders!" Velma explains.

"Genius! Let's get started," Daphne says.

The kids use the metal tent poles as struts and braces for the gliders. Then they stretch the canvas over the structures to create wings. It does not take long to build five simple hang gliders.

"These aren't going to win any prizes for looks, but they'll get the job done," Velma says when they've finished.

"Like, isn't it dangerous to fly these in this storm?" Shaggy trembles.

"Not as dangerous as getting caught by those guys!" Daphne says and points to a pack of Yeti guards coming at them.

Turn to page 98.

Shaggy and Scooby land on the conveyor belt and start running.

"Like, why aren't we going anywhere?" Shaggy wonders aloud. Scooby points down at the conveyor belt. They are running against its forward motion. "Oops!"

Shaggy and Scooby turn around and run as fast as they can. Stuffed toys go flying into the air. So do the diamonds. The workers scramble to grab the gems. Shaggy and Scooby escape.

"Quick! Hide in that crate!" Shaggy says. The pals jump into a big wooden box full of stuffed toys and shut the lid.

Turn to page 92.

"Zoinks! We're moving!" Shaggy says as the crate gets lifted from the ground. Then it is loaded on a lorry, which drives off. "We're leaving!"

Shaggy and Scooby peek out of the crate. They are outside on a mountain road.

"Like, the blizzard stopped. Now we can look for Daphne, Velma, and Fred. Let's go, Scoob!" Shaggy says. They jump out of the crate and off the lorry.

The vehicle drives away down the mountain. Shaggy and Scooby are left standing in the snow in the middle of nowhere.

"Maybe we jumped too soon. It's going to be a long walk back to the village," Shaggy moans.

THE END

To follow another path, turn to page 11.

"I really didn't think you kids would make it down the mountain alive," the man says. "You are very resourceful. But that won't help you now."

"Hey, I know you," Fred realizes. "I saw you in the office talking to Bigfoot back in the United States."

"Yes. I ran that operation until you kids interfered," the man says. "We had to shut it down before the authorities arrived."

"So here you are in Tibet using Yetis to scare the locals instead of Bigfoot," Velma states.

"It's Granddad's idea," the man reveals with a shrug. "You can ask him all the questions you want when you see him."

Turn to page 97.

Scooby ignores Shaggy's warning and leaps out of the cart. Shaggy quickly follows. The two watch the cart fall into the mine shaft behind them.

"Way to go, Scooby!" Shaggy exclaims. "Like, for once, I'm glad you didn't listen to me."

"Re roo!" Scooby replies, kissing the ground at his feet. **MWAH! MWAH!**

"Now let's find a way out of here," Shaggy says, scanning the area.

"Ris ray," Scooby suggests and points to a tunnel.

The two friends start walking. Soon, they see a light at the end of the tunnel.

"A way out! We're saved!" Shaggy exclaims.

"Ruh-roh," Scooby gulps.

"It's a dead end," Shaggy says.

The tunnel ends high up in a larger cave. The light is coming from big floodlights that illuminate an underground factory.

"Aww, they're making stuffed animals," Shaggy observes. "Wait. They're putting something inside the toys besides stuffing."

"Riamonds!" Scooby exclaims, spotting piles and piles of the sparkling jewels.

"It's a smuggling operation," Shaggy realizes. "I'll bet it's connected to the Bigfoot scheme back home."

Just then, a big, hairy hand grips Shaggy on the shoulder. He turns and comes face to face with a Yeti!

ROOOOOARRRR!

The giant beast lets out a terrifying wail with his hot breath.

"Zoinks!" Shaggy shrieks.

"Reah," Scooby says, plugging his nose. "Try a reath rint."

"Come on, Scoobs!" shouts Shaggy. He and Scooby jump and fall into giant bin of toy stuffing. The Yeti follows them.

Turn the page.

When they emerge from the bottom, Shaggy and Scooby realize the Yeti's head has fallen off!

"Hey, that was just a mask! You're a man, not a monster," Shaggy says.

The fake Yeti tries to grab Scooby and Shaggy, but they scamper over him and out of the bin.

Turn to page 90.

Shaggy, Scooby, Fred, Daphne, and Velma are marched by the Yeti guards towards a helicopter. They climb inside. The interior is very luxurious, but they don't feel very comfortable. The guards tie them up with rope.

"Where are we going?" Daphne asks.

"You'll see when you get there," the man replies. He settles into a seat and buckles the seat belt. "It will be the last thing you see."

Turn to page 101.

The kids grab the hang gliders and launch into the air. They don't have time to think about the possible dangers. Real danger is coming at them on snowmobiles. The Yeti guards shoot their stun rifles but miss.

ZAP! ZAP! ZAP!

The wind catches the canvas wings of the gliders and tosses the frail contraptions like bits of confetti. Updrafts hurl them high in the air. Downdrafts plunge them towards the ground. The kids can barely control their creations.

"Head down into the valley! The air will be calmer there," Velma instructs. She just hopes it's true.

Turn to page 100.

The gang circles over Chatang village. They've been knocked around by the fierce winds. Their hang gliders are coming apart, but they manage to land. Shaggy and Scooby scramble out of the tattered gliders and kiss the ground.

"Safe at last!" Shaggy sighs.

"Not quite, you meddling kids," a voice declares. A tall man walks towards the gang. There are a dozen Yeti guards behind him.

"Re're roomed," Scooby whimpers.

Turn to page 93.

The helicopter lands at a remote airport in the Himalaya Mountains. Yeti guards move Scooby-Doo and the gang to a private jet. The aircraft is even more luxurious than the helicopter.

"Like, wherever we're going, it's first class all the way," Shaggy comments.

"More rike a rast meal," Scooby gulps.

"I'm hungry!" Shaggy says. "Can a guy get something to eat around here?"

A pretty flight attendant puts a tray filled with food in front of Shaggy and his friends.

"Thank you," Daphne says politely to the woman. "You're very kind, even if you do work for global smugglers."

The flight attendant does not reply. She smiles as the kids eat the food.

SNORE!

Scooby and the gang are fast asleep.

"The sleep aid in the food worked. It's time to take off," the attendant tells the pilot.

Turn the page.

Next, she speaks into a mobile phone to a distant listener. "We're on our way."

Many hours later, the kids wake up. They are in a fabulous house in tropical surroundings. Guards stand at the only door. They look like Bigfoot!

"It looks like we're back where we started," Fred says.

"No, you're in the Everglades in Florida, USA," a voice corrects Fred. "We don't use Bigfoot or Yetis here. This is Swamp Ape territory."

The kids turn to see a gaunt old man. He is as tall as Bigfoot and his hair and beard are as white as a Yeti!

Turn to page 104.

"You're Granddad!" Velma realizes. She studies the old man's resemblance to the legendary Bigfoot and Yeti. Then she understands. "You used Bigfoot and the Yeti to scare people because you resembled the creatures!"

"Yes!" Granddad admits. "I grew up resenting those monsters, but now I use them to my advantage."

"So, everywhere there's a legend of a big hairy monster, it's you?" Shaggy asks.

"It's a cover for one of my smuggling operations, yes," Granddad replies. "We use the Yowie in Australia, Sasquatch in Canada, and the Swamp Ape here in Florida."

"Jeepers, that's a lot of monsters," Daphne says.

"It's also a perfect confession," Velma says. She talks into a microphone hidden in her clothing. "Did you get that Agent Dinkley?"

"What?!" Granddad exclaims.

"You're wired?" he says. "Why didn't anyone check these meddling kids for listening devices?"

"I'm also equipped with a handy-dandy tracking device, thanks to my cousin in Interpol," Velma reveals. "The task force should be here any minute."

They hear the sound of helicopters approaching. The guards run. Granddad is left standing alone.

"My operation is ruined!" the old man laments.

"And another mystery is solved!" Fred exclaims. "It's time for a victory cheer."

"Scooby-Dooby-Doo!" they all shout!

THE END

To follow another path, turn to page 11.

AUTHOR

Laurie S. Sutton has read comics since she was a kid. She grew up to become an editor for Marvel, DC Comics, Starblaze, and Tekno Comics. She has written Adam Strange for DC, Star Trek: Voyager for Marvel, plus Star Trek: Deep Space Nine and Witch Hunter for Malibu Comics. There are large boxes of comics in her wardrobe where there should be clothing and shoes. Laurie has lived all over the world. She currently resides in Florida, USA.

ILLUSTRATOR

Scott Neely has been a professional illustrator and designer for many years. For the last eight years, he's been an official Scooby-Doo and Cartoon Network artist, working on such licenced properties as Dexter's Laboratory, Johnny Bravo, Courage The Cowardly Dog, Powerpuff Girls, and more. He has also worked on Pokemon, Mickey Mouse Clubhouse, My Friends Tigger & Pooh, Handy Manny, Strawberry Shortcake, Bratz, and many other popular characters. He lives in a suburb of Philadelphia, USA, and has a scrappy Yorkshire Terrier, Alfie.

GLOSSARY

dangerous (DAYN-jur-uhs) – likely to cause harm or injury

diversion (di-VUR-zhuhn) – something that distracts

frail (FRAYL) – weak

illuminates (i-LOO-muh-nates) – brings to light

impostor (im-PO-stur) – someone who pretends to be someone that he or she is not

intruder (in-TROOD-ur) – a person who goes into a place or gets involved in a situation where he or she is not wanted

meddling (MED-ling) – getting involved in someone else's personal business

propellers (pruh-PEL-urs) – a set of rotating blades that provide force to move an object through air or water

smugglers (SMUHG-lurs) – people who move goods into or out of a place illegally

texture (TEKS-chur) – the structure, feel, or appearance of something

vortex (VOR-teks) – the centre of a mass of swirling fluid, towards which things are drawn

What do you give Big Foot for dinner?
a. **Spag-yeti.**
b. **Sasquatch-amole and chips.**
c. **Plenty of room!**

What do you find under Big Foot's feet?
a. **Lint from his big footie pyjamas.**
b. **Surprised campers.**
c. **Why are you even getting that close? Gross!**

What does Big Foot have that no other monster has?
a. **Big toes.**
b. **The world's worst case of athlete's foot.**
c. **Little Bigfoots!**

Why did Scooby play Frisbee with the bear?
a. He thought it was a cub scout.
b. He wanted to see a cub and saucer.
c. He likes playing catch bear-handed.

What do you get if you cross Big Foot with a kangaroo?
a. A furry coat with pockets!
b. A furry coat that can bounce!
c. Big shoes with lots of spring in their step!

Why does a young Big Foot do when his feet are tired?
a. Calls a toe truck.
b. Says, "The shoe must go on!"
c. Eats his vegetables so he can grow another foot!

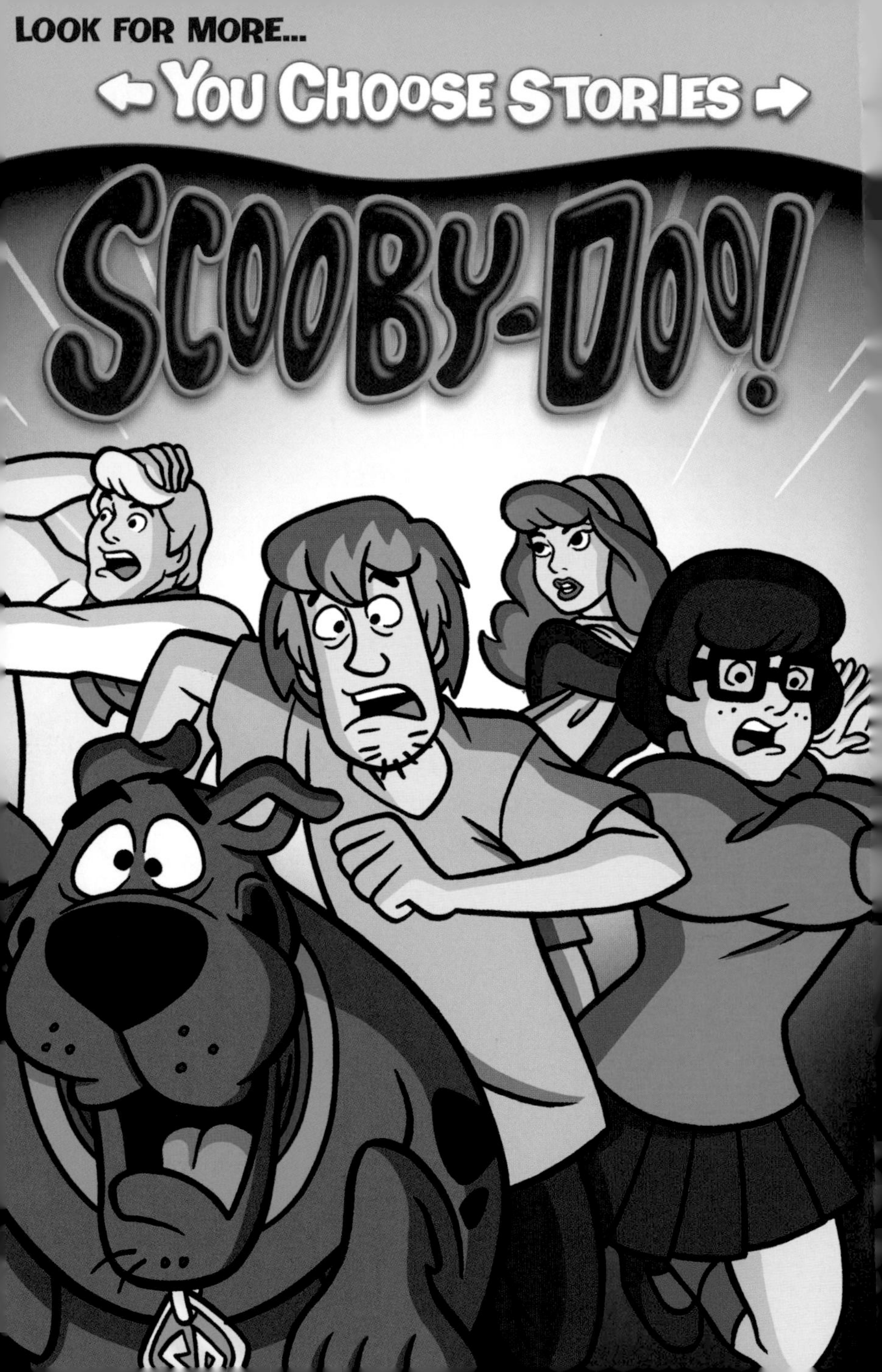
LOOK FOR MORE...
YOU CHOOSE STORIES
SCOOBY-DOO!

THE CHOICE IS YOURS!